Wind, Light, and the Twenty-Year-Old Me

SAKAGUCHI ANGO

Translated by

MAPLOPO

Copyright © 2022 Maplopo

All rights reserved. No part of this publication may
be reproduced, stored in a retrieval system or
transmitted in any form or by any means, electronic,
mechanical, photocopying, recording or otherwise,
without prior permission of Maplopo.

ISBN: 978-4-9911255-2-2

DEDICATION

For all those who help us grow.

CONTENTS

Introduction from Doc and Reiko   i

Wind, Light, and the Twenty-Year-Old Me   1

Aftertalk   24

The Life of Sakaguchi Ango: 40
biographical timeline

INTRODUCTION FROM DOC & REIKO...

What is unhappiness? What does it mean to be unhappy? And can settling into it, breathing it in, enduring its weight upon us until we finally pass through it, actually be the answer to knowing its polar opposite? For Sakaguchi Ango, the answer to this last question would be an emphatic yes. To the first two, it would seem he never gave up the personal quest to find out.

Today, if you were to ask someone if they know what it feels like to be unhappy, they'd likely tell you they're far too acquainted with it, that it is the shadow that trails them day in and day out. Adults in particular suffer from this malaise, but so do younger adults, teens and even toddlers; so one must assume if given the ability to vocalize their distress beyond their bleating, they would share the same sentiment. Joy is what we seek. Unhappiness we've had enough of for the moment.

Strangely, through Sakaguchi Ango's lens, surface level happiness is what we need to flee from. We're too happy, too content—misguided. To rescue ourselves, we should seek and swim through the depths of despair, because only after that can we later break through to the surface of life. "Rise up, Japan!" he shouts in his masterful, 1946 essay, "Discourse on Decadence." He sees opportunity on the horizon as Japan pulls itself out from the wretched beauty of war, and he wants us to listen.

A year later, he infuses the idea in his beautiful, complicated telling of his younger years, far too happy a youngster lying in the wheat fields and sloshing through the swamps in the outskirts of Tokyo in the early part of the twentieth century.

INTRODUCTION FROM DOC & REIKO

It's a Tokyo filled with pit vipers (imagine!) and all manner of human characters who intrigue, annoy and depress Ango; we're treated to self-absorbed teachers, sly, mischievous children (with whom Ango particularly relates), an old man of a certain influence who looks to exploit his position and finesse his way into the life of a local beauty, parents so reluctant to recognize their own frailties they thrust those inadequacies upon their children, and three very special, and very troubled girls, that for Ango, serve as his first real introduction into the meaning of true unhappiness.

While *Wind, Light, and the Twenty-Year-Old Me*, is a relatively short work, translating it was hardly a walk in the park. Famously, his "Discourse on Decadence" required a sequel of sorts in the form of the more direct, "Discourse on Decadence, Part II" as a reply to readers who weren't quite understanding where he was coming from in the first writing. Ango is indeed vague even when he's writing in Japanese, and maintaining his voice and vision as he contemplates, criticizes, and expounds upon life as a Buddhist monk might, was a task which took us many weeks and months to perfect.

The coincidence of Reiko growing up in a temple family provides much in the way of perspective when we need to dig deep into some Japanese storytelling, and with the publication of Nakajima's *Legend of the Master* in 2020, and this one from Sakaguchi, we've certainly found ourselves deep in the mire of Buddhist thinking. Ango, we think, would be pleased that we dug as deeply as we did, and that we were stuck as often as we were. Or, would he?

From the outside, it's difficult to tell. Because while it may seem the young Ango we meet at the outset of *Wind and Light* is as pleased as punch with life as one could be, it's also clear deep down he is quite disappointed with the complacency that accompanies that outward smile. It's the pain that lies beneath the smile that's most intriguing to Ango (and most encouraging it would seem), and he would probably be more excited to hear how much of a pain in the keister he was to understand, rather than how much we learned from reading and translating the story. After all, pain is good, right? Saying it was fun would be a lie, of course (it wasn't), and, well, Ango isn't too fond of that sort of thing. So, we won't lie to you. Ango was incredible. But, hard. We should all suffer, he'd say. It's better that way.

And suffering is precisely what some of his characters in *Wind and Light* are forced to endure. Particularly, the three young girls at the heart of the story that serve as life instructors to Ango as he comes to know them as a substitute teacher in 1925. Not so many years their senior at the time, it doesn't take much for Ango to see the pained, stressful lives they live, and yet he observes them quite agnostically, somehow understanding their fate is somewhat inescapable, as is fate for most humans, unaware as to what they're missing. This is not an easy idea to grasp.

In "Discourse on Decadence," Ango mentions a niece who committed suicide—a beautiful, but sad girl, who ends her life before reaching her twenties. Maybe it was a good thing, a younger Ango wonders for a moment, for she succeeded in preserving herself for eternity as a thing of beauty. But he also contemplates whether he could have protected her from this inevitable "fall." To a wiser, older Ango, she effectively gave into her frailty instead of crawling through the pain so she could come out of it at the end. He views her as having given up (in the same way he was critical of Dazai's penchant for suicide attempts, and eventual success).

Ango's encouragement to live a full life is mirrored with complexity, and is difficult to interpret, but it's there in the re-reading, in the pulling apart of the text, in the consulting with others who know more than us. Understanding how he believes we can get there is even more convoluted to the modern mind, more so to the western mind, it seems, and reading Ango's thoughts on all this is very much like being lost in a Buddhist Koan—everything he says is a study in contrasts. Even Ango himself appears to be stuck in the Koan as well. And, he's okay with that. It's part of the process. He takes swipes at his neighbors, and he takes swipes at himself. He's hard on everyone.

INTRODUCTION FROM DOC & REIKO

He's like the coach who drives us to exhaustion and pain in practice so when game time arrives it doesn't hurt as much. He's not afraid to call us idiots for wanting to hide from pain, not afraid to empathize with us when we complain about it (and occasionally join us), and not afraid to call our bluff when we're pretending to enjoy our sedated life, while at the same time being aware he shutters some of his own desires. To be human, after all, is to be human. He knows growth is only experienced through suffering, and yet he's fully aware that pushing beyond those setbacks is the most difficult part of living—for everyone. It's a beautiful thing, and Ango does indeed see beauty everywhere, even in our human frailties. They serve a purpose. It's only when we hide them away that we fail to live. And that, ultimately, is what is most important.

"Kaze to hikari to hatachi no watashi to" (Wind, light, and the twenty-year-old me) was published in January of 1947, a few months after Ango turned the corner on forty. Given the depth of the story, it's fair to assume the effort of taking pen to paper was the result of introspection decades in the making. A large family, multiple father figures, the loss of many friends at an early age, war... trauma, and tests of endurance were ever-present for many in Japan at the time—many throughout the world, for that matter.

Still, Ango was hardly caught up on this, and in no way one-dimensional. He had fun too. And, a lot of it. There's this wonderful picture of Ango in Roger Pulvers' article entitled, "Refilling the Glass: Sakaguchi Ango's Legacy"; he's smiling gleefully, caught in a haze of motion, laughing with his young boy, Tsunao, perched on his lap and his dog aiming for a lick at his face. He's happy. Who wouldn't be? It's a wonderful picture to swap out in your mind with the one we see everywhere. You know... the shot with Ango sitting in his room at that low table... discarded paper crumpled up and tossed about so haphazardly it appears he'll soon be swallowed up. That one. Here at Maplopo, we prefer to think of Ango laughing a lot. Certainly possible. After all, the funniest people always pull successfully from pain. And because of that, we like to think of Ango with a bit more cheer in him—almost like the Buddy Christ character in Kevin Smith's film, Dogma. Or to go back even further, to Willis Wheatley's 1973 iconic "Christ, Liberator" painting, better known as "Laughing Jesus."

So, a happier Ango than even he'd like to admit—without the fear of contentment, without the angst. Just happy. Simply, a sweet hearted, brilliant man, in round spectacles, who thinks it must be better to be *unhappy* because he just might be the only one who's gone deep enough to discover the secret to happiness long before the rest of us catch on.

Doc and Reiko Kane
Co-founders, Maplopo
February 14, 2022 Kobe, Japan

WIND, LIGHT, AND THE TWENTY-YEAR-OLD ME

Having been expelled from school and needing to repeat a grade, I was twenty years old when I graduated from high school. My old man died when I was eighteen, and after discovering all he left for us was debt, we moved into a row house. People around me said it would be nonsense for a person like me who hates studying to go to university. And, even though they weren't really telling me not to go to university, it made sense. So, I decided to work instead. I became a substitute teacher.

By nature, I give myself license to do things at whim; with my natural disposition, it's impossible for me to obey the orders of others. I had developed a taste for skipping classes ever since I was a kindergartener, and during my middle and high school years, I skipped at least half my classes. I would leave all my textbooks at my school desk, and when I went to school, carried nothing with me; it wasn't like I went to movies or any other fun places while not attending school. In my middle school years, all I did was lie on the sand dune along the shore in my hometown, surrounded by pine trees, gazing idly at the ocean and the sky; in particular, I wasn't reading novels or any other written materials. I was entirely squandering time—my fate throughout life. I was expelled from that countryside school and transferred to a school in Tokyo where there was a fair number of delinquent boys. Even there I remained king of absences, and rarely went to the movies or anywhere else; I could often be found lying in the cemetery behind the school, or nearby in the prisoners' cemetery, a meadow of 990 square meters surrounded by trees that lay just beyond another graveyard, the Zōshigaya Cemetery. It was very common for me to lie on my back idling in the meadow, and have my fellow truants visit in search of me. We had a famous boxer at the time, S, in the same grade. He would skip school and show up with his boxing gloves, and we'd spar in the meadow. Back then, I had a weak stomach as I do now, and getting punched in the gut meant an instant knockout on my end, so I didn't box. The shadowy area beneath the trees in the meadow was swampy and filled with snakes, so the boxer said he was going to catch and sell the snakes, and took some home; once I went to his house to hang out, and he was keeping snakes in the drawer of his desk. One day, the boxer found a snake in the prisoners' cemetery, leapt upon it, grabbed it by the tail and dangled it in the air. Immediately, he realized the snake was a pit viper, and out of sheer terror went into a sudden frenzy whipping it round and round in circles with maniacal earnestness; he kept whipping it about without a single utterance for a good five minutes. Then he dashed it against the ground and crushed its head under foot; strangely, I remember clearly to this day him painstakingly crushing the snake's head and muttering, "F that. Bitten by a pit viper in a prisoners' cemetery and dead—in no way would that be funny."

    I did a translation for him once at his request. He wrote literary miscellany about boxing for several magazines, and had me translate a boxing novel into Japanese for publication in *Shinseinen*. "How to Win the Hearts of the People" was the title, and that was what I translated.[1] The pay was three yen per submission, and he said he would give me half the manuscript fee, but later waffled and never even gave me a sliver of that amount. Later in life, after becoming a paid writer, even first-rate magazines only paid two yen, or two yen fifty sen at most, and not until about fifteen years had passed in my life as a writer would I come to earn three yen per submission. Income derived from pure literature is a far cry from that offered up for the poorly written translation of a high schooler.

After enrolling as a student at this school filled with delinquent boys, I developed a vague aspiration for religion. A person like me who cannot obey the orders of others may perhaps find significant pleasure in obeying his own restrictive commands. But, my yearning was fundamentally ambiguous, and I was feeling something like a nostalgia for the austerity of ascetic practice.

It might sound strange for a former delinquent unable to follow school rules to become an elementary school substitute teacher, but as an impressionable youngster I had hopes and aspirations common for that age; besides, I was much more mature back then than I am now. These days, I have become the sort of person who cannot adequately engage in even normal social interactions, but when young, I possessed moderation and manners, and putting on airs, I would speak with parents as if I were some kind of respected educator.

A lawyer in Niigata, named Ban Jun was writing for *Kaizou* and others back then, and being a dreamer, built a shack deep in the mountains in Ōume and lived a primitive life with his wife. I later rented the shack, and lived there as well at one point; when I was there I was troubled by snakes that would enter the shack because I was eating flying squirrels I'd hunted with bow and arrow. When I became a teacher, Mr. Ban taught me the following: "When talking with someone, first, begin speaking in a soft voice. Have a listener go, 'What? What was that?' and prick up the person's ears in order to first pull the person in."

There is an eccentric artist of Japanese paintings in my school district, who draws nothing but catfish and has deformed three-fingered hands; his name is Fujita and he is a friend of Mr. Ban. "Fujita has a unique state of mind, so why don't you visit him?" Ban said, and provided me with a letter of introduction. So I paid him a visit. "I just came to give my greetings today. I'll come back in the near future when things are a little less pressing," I said, but he demanded, "No, stop saying such things. We've got soda here. Come on in!" He was adamant about me coming inside; "Okay, then," I surrendered, and entered the house. Then I heard him calling out to his wife and ordering her, "Hey, go buy soda!"; this had me bewildered.

My place of work as a substitute was Setagaya, Shimokitazawa, which used to be named Ebara-gun, an utter wilderness like Musashino; after quitting my teaching post, Odakyū Electric Railway was constructed and opened to traffic, but when I was there the area was engulfed in bamboo groves. Located next to Setagaya Town Hall was the main school; the branch school where I worked had no more than three classrooms. In front of the school, there was a temple referred to as Awashima-sama, famous for moxibustion or something, and next to the school, there was a shop that sold school supplies, bread, and candies, but other than that, the surroundings were just an absolutely boundless expanse of fields; needless to say, there was no bus back then. I believe it might be around where Inoue Tomoichirō lives now, but so much has changed since then, and I can no longer place it. At the time, not even a farmhouse neighbored the school; the surrounding area was just an expanse of absolute wilderness, with hills extending in one direction populated by thickets of bamboo and fields of wheat, and there was a primeval forest too. They called it Mamoriyama Park, but it was far from being a park; it was just a primeval forest where I would often take children and let them play.

I taught fifth grade, the eldest group at the branch school, a total of about seventy boys and girls; I wouldn't be surprised if those too much to handle were pushed from the main campus to the branch school. Of the seventy, about twenty could barely manage to write their names in *katakana*, but beyond that, they couldn't write one simple *konnichiwa*. A good twenty of them. That group was always fighting in the classroom, and there was this one kid, who if he heard soldiers passing by singing a war song outside the building, would leap from the classroom window and go watch the soldiers. That kid was ferocious and abnormal. He was the child of a clam selling family. When cholera was prevalent and their clams could not be sold anymore, he said, "Hell, no! My clams cannot be beaten by damn cholera!" and ate the clams; each member of his family was infected with cholera. The kid would vomit white stuff that looked like rice soup on the way to school. His entire family narrowly escaped death, though.

Truly adorable kids exist among the ones that are considered bad. Children are all adorable, of course, but beautiful souls reside within the naughty ones. The naughty ones have warm hearts and an appreciation for the nostalgic. These kids should not be forced to study subjects which give them a headache; instead, we should nurture character traits that allow them to be warm-hearted and nostalgic—traits they can rely on to live strong. Having those principles, I did not care if they were not able to write words in *hiragana* or *katakana*. There was a milk house boy called Tanaka; he milked the cows both day and night, and delivered milk on his own. At some point in the past, he had apparently failed to advance to the next grade, so he was a year older than the other students in his class. When I first arrived at the school as a substitute, the head teacher told me to keep a particular eye on him because he was strong and bullied other children; true as that may have been, he was, however, a very nice kid. Whenever I visited his house asking if I could see him milk the cows, he came out jumping, overjoyed. Sometimes he did bully other children, but offered a hand with physically strenuous jobs such as cleaning up the ditches or carrying stuff, and did everything on his own without fooling around. He would beg adorably, "Teacher, I can't write words, but please don't scold me. Instead, I'll do any sort of labor work." I can't comprehend why an adorable child like him is notoriously labeled as a bad student; under no circumstances should a child be reprimanded solely because he's unable to write letters. It's a child's soul that matters most. It's outrageous to flunk a student because the child cannot write.

I was stumped by girls. By the fifth grade or so they were already women, and among those I knew, there were two that had me wondering if they weren't physiologically women already.

At first I lived in the only boarding house nearby school; there were not many rooms, so I had to lodge with another person. A practical school for overseas colonization was nearby, so I lodged with a student from the Tōhoku region, an absolute country bumpkin from a farmer family, and an odd man who didn't eat warm meals.[2] Having done farm work since childhood, and growing up eating only cold meals, he said he couldn't possibly bring himself to eat warm meals, and would let food cool down before eating. The daughter of the boarding family, though, who was twenty-four or twenty-five, and a big woman who looked like she weighed as much as seventy-five kilograms was quite taken with me, and she came to my room to hang around... boy, she'd be all excited and fluttered, filled with infatuation, slurring her words..., her facial features softening and the outer corners of her eyes dipping downward in adoration..., fidgety, entirely jittery and talking..., silent, and grinning; this sudden attack of hers would leave me nonplussed. She'd continually bring warm rice exclusively to my room after cooking it herself and caused my fellow roommate, Mr. Nekojita, to lament his fate.[3] Without a way to deal with this daughter's state of fervent love, the old married couple who ran the boarding house seemed entirely at a loss, but I was more perplexed than they were, and moved out after about twenty days. When I disclosed to them my decision to move out, saying I couldn't get any studying done while sharing a room with another lodger, I found their state of

WIND, LIGHT, AND THE TWENTY-YEAR-OLD ME

relief unexpected, and their gratitude beyond even all imagination. From that moment onward, it seemed this old married couple endlessly praised and applauded me in the most elevated way possible—which wouldn't even have occurred to me—but would you believe, another daughter from the boarding house was a student of mine, the most precocious of the bunch; she found their praise disappointing because she never anticipated her parents would praise me, and to my face said, "It's strange my father and mother praise you so much." "You are not that nice," she said. With these girls, my partiality to boy brats was seen as unexpected and caused jealousy and feelings of betrayal. The intensity of the envy exhibited by the girls was a revelation to me seeing it for the first time at twenty, and I was utterly perplexed to come up with countermeasures.

I moved into a place on the second floor of a house owned by the branch school's head teacher. It was located in Daitabashi, just over four kilometers from the school. Half the children attending the branch school walked roughly the same distance, though, so prior to arriving, about thirty students and I would end up walking together. Sometimes, I would be a bit behind, and there would be a student who would say things with a mischievous grin like: "Oh, it's natural—you're young. Where did you end up sleeping last night?" All these children helped with the farming once home from school, so even though they couldn't write katakana, they were mature for their age.

As a side job, the head teacher had a teacher board with him. The prior border was another substitute teacher, a Mr. Nagaoka, who was later transferred to the main school. He was an avid reader of Russian literature and quite an oddball. He had a peculiar disease called frog epileptic seizure, and whenever he saw a frog he went into convulsions. A year before, when my class was in the fourth grade and taught by Mr. Nagaoka, one of the students hid a frog in his chalk box. Upon discovering this during class, Mr. Nagaoka apparently toppled over and foam began bubbling from his mouth; the milk house boy recounted this story to me and said, "At the time, I was so startled." I thought perhaps it could have been him. I asked, "Wasn't it you who did it?" He said, "No, not me—," with a cute, meaningful smirk.

The head teacher was about sixty years old, but with unbounded energy; unusually short at 140 centimeters, but with a wide, muscular build, and although he was hiding it beneath his mustache, he had a harelip. He had a fiery temper and damned those around him left and right, perhaps a result of some underlying cowardice. He leaned especially hard on the janitor and students, but when it came to school board members or influential people in the village, he went right into brown-nosing them; whenever he lost his temper, he would push the responsibility of teaching class to the old teacher in charge of the first graders, venturing off instead to an influential person's house to chit-chat over tea. Regardless, for us teachers, we were more pleased not to have him at school anyways, so we didn't complain about having his responsibilities imposed on us in this way. On those occasions when he did get fiery mad, he walloped and kicked his wife hard, and after all that, he would charge out of his house into a grove of mixed trees or a bamboo forest, and recklessly hit tree trunks or bamboo with his walking stick. That was plain insanity, and I wondered if his hands did not hurt using such tremendous power, but he totally immersed himself in the hitting for five minutes or so, shouting "Ei! Ei! Ei! Yah! Yah! Yah!"

"These youngsters… greenhorns…" was the head teacher's disdainful and typical reference toward young people, but I was not in the slightest affected by these slurs, because those days I held myself entirely aloof from worldly stuff, emotionally distancing myself from feelings of anger, sadness, hatred, or joy; I tried to live life allowing nature to take its course and didn't fuss about anything, like a cloud drifting in the sky or water floating with the tide. He often excluded me from his damning, though, because he feared not collecting rent if he were to get mad at me and I moved out; he was cunning like that. Including me and the head teacher, there were a total of five teachers: the first grade male teacher, old Yamakado, the second grade female teacher, Fukuhara, and the third grade female teacher, Ishige. Mr. Yamakado was reclusive like me, maybe sixty-five years old, and walked to school all the way from Asabu wearing straw sandals. Apparently, he had coerced his daughter into working as a teacher in the city, and she wanted to get married at some point in the near future, but no-no, Mr. Yamakado would not allow that; he needed her to help with the family's finances a bit longer. Every day he argued with her about it, and every day he told us about it: "Oh my, that young one has awakened to sex or something. She sure is itching to be married. Ah, ha, ha, ha!" He had ten children, which caused his household to be in dire straits, and he entrusted his entire well-being to a little 180 milliliter flask of sake that he got to drink each night. The head teacher did not drink.

There is a strange inversion to the moral sense of elementary school teachers. That is, because they perceive educators as being mentors, they strive to live a life abstinent of vulgar behavior to avoid criticism from others, while assuming regular people remain indifferent to this standard and carelessly indulge in all manner of wicked behavior, which consequently allows them to think, "We can also be allowed a little bit of vice," and to partake in bad deeds. They assume: "Other people are doing far worse things than what I'm doing. What I'm doing is not that big a deal"; however, in reality, they do things so crooked as to be beyond the realm of possibility for others. This tendency exists among rural villagers as well; they assume: "City dwellers are bad, and always up to wrongdoing, so we should be allowed a certain degree of misdeed." In actuality, they end up doing things far more crooked than what city dwellers are doing. The same too goes for religionists. I think it's inherently wrong to reflect upon the way others think and act, instead of thinking and acting on one's own; but what's worse is their reflection overall is delusive. It would surprise me that the teachers went overboard in imagining and interpreting human society as being so evil and vulgar.

The first time I visited the main school after having received official notification of my appointment, a female teacher there informed me I'd be working at the branch school, and because she lived in the area, offered to escort me to the building. She was stunningly beautiful. I had never seen such a beautiful woman until that very moment, and for the first time realized there existed a kind of beauty that could snap one straight. She was twenty-seven, single, and I heard through the grapevine she intended to remain single for life. She seemed to have a sturdy conviction which made her appear incredibly noble, modest, kind, and feminine—different from that common, "neutral" female teacher type. I secretly held deep admiration for her. There was very little contact between the main campus and the branch school, so we had no real chance of conversing after that; still, I embraced an impression of her as something noble for the next few years.

There was a wealthy, influential man in our village, and though he was quite old, he wanted to marry this teacher and make her his second wife, his first wife having died. He asked the head teacher for a favor in this matter. The promised reward was said to have been a few hundred, or a few thousand yen, and what a sight it was to see this head teacher bustling about, leaving his class unattended; it was all fruitless because the person at the heart of the matter, the female teacher, had no intention whatsoever of being married anyway. Every day the head teacher took his frustration out on everyone, and we took pains handling this man's rough, or rather frenzied temper for a month or two.

I was not particularly planning to, nor wanting to, confess my love to the female teacher, or get married to her for that matter; I was simply happy to hold the dear memory of her in my mind because, after all, my motto was "let nature take its course and don't be attached to anything," but when I heard of the head teacher's maneuvering, I was very anxious thinking my vision of the beautiful woman could be crushed by such an offensive marriage; I came to secretly despise him regardless of this façade of mine about letting nature take its course.

One of my other colleagues, Mrs. Ishige, was the wife of a military police sergeant major or something along those lines, a really cold, neutral-type of person while another colleague, Ms. Fukuhara, was a nice aunty-type. She was probably thirty-five or six, and was the type of person who devoted herself to students, giving no care to her appearance. Her innate disposition was more like that of a kindergarten teacher than a middle school teacher. Despite being single, she didn't have the bitchy quality of neutral-type women; she didn't have any lofty ideals or anything, but she was a nice person. For me it was a pleasant fact that she was the noble teacher's best friend and had a worshipful kind of respect toward her. Many female teachers were jealous of the noble teacher. When I was leaving my teaching job, she said, "It is hard and sad to see you leave, but it is a good thing. You really should not remain a teacher and live out your life being just that." She congratulated me, made a bounty of food, and held a farewell feast. I was, however, feeling sad about my ambition which made it impossible for me to settle for a teaching job. Why could I not dedicate myself to being a teacher?

I used to enjoy lingering in the staff room by myself after school. With all the students gone and the teachers no longer there, it was just me sitting absorbed in thought. There was only the sound of the wall clock. The fact that the hustle and bustle of the schoolyard turned to complete emptiness—no sounds, no people—mysteriously made the stillness come to the fore; it was oddly hollow, and in this state of absent-mindedness, it was as though I had disappeared to somewhere else. In the midst of being absorbed by this vacant feeling, I came to imagine an apparition of myself sticking out its neck from the shadow of the clock on the wall and saying hello. I'd suddenly catch myself seeing myself, and I felt like my apparition was standing next to me and speaking to me, "Hey, what's going on?" Although I liked having my mind in a dull haze, sometimes my apparition would unexpectedly appear next to me like this and nag: "Hey, you! Don't be so satisfied," he'd say, glaringly.

"I can't be satisfied?"

"Of course not. You must suffer. You must make yourself suffer as much as you can."

"For what?"

"You suffer, and only through that suffering will you be shown the answer. A person's nobility lies in having oneself suffer. Everybody prefers being satisfied, even a beast."

Is this true, I thought? The possible veracity of what my apparition was saying aside, I certainly did indulge in satisfaction. Truly, I was coming close to becoming like a Zen monk, allowing nature to take its course and living without attachments; instances where I'd become angry, happy, or sad came about less and less, and I seemed to have much more composure, maturity, and comprehension of things than did fifty- and sixty-year-old teachers despite being merely twenty. Generally, I did not have a desire for possessions. I did not wish for my soul to be limited. In summer or winter, I wore the same clothes throughout the year, I gave away books once I finished reading them, and a few changes of clothes, shirts and *fundoshi*, were my only surplus possessions; a parent who visited me one day spread a funny narrative that I hung my fundoshi on the wall just like any other article of clothing. "Oh really?" I thought, "Is it only me who does this?" My surprise was greater than theirs. Hanging my fundoshi was purely my way of keeping tidy. There was no concept of storage in my spirit, so of course no closet was needed. The only thing I stored as my possession was a vision of the noble female teacher; the reason I was reading the Bible around that time was because I was pleasantly associating the image of her with the Virgin Mary. Admittedly, I admired this female teacher, and yet, I was not in love with her. Not in the slightest did I feel as though I might lose my balance over her as if I were in love. All I wished for was the chance to at least sit next to her while working in the staff room at school. Today, no longer do I own the image of her in my heart. I cannot even recall her face, nor do I remember her name.

WIND, LIGHT, AND THE TWENTY-YEAR-OLD ME

★

Those days, I felt as though there was a life force in the sun and I saw boundless effervescence and waves of æther in the rays it cast. A mere glance upward to the blue sky to soak up its light left me content. Being carefree, and having the wind and light sweep through the wheat fields, gave me the utmost pleasure.

I could gaze at life so dear within every single drop of rain on a rainy day and within the sound of the madly screaming wind on a stormy day. I continued feeling this precious life in the leaves of trees, birds, insects, and those clouds that drifted above—always chatting with my heart. Since there was nothing at all prompting me to drink alcohol, I never considered enjoying it. I was satisfied with the mere vision of that graceful female teacher, so I did not need the flesh of a woman. At night, I was tired, and so I slept well.

The distance between nature and myself gradually narrowed, and my senses bathed with satisfaction in nature's touch and life force. Experiencing this wasn't directly triggering any anxiety for me, but sure enough, when feeling content, walking along the crest of a wheat field, or through a thick, dark, primeval forest, I again began to encounter, out of the blue, an apparition of myself; I'd see it speaking to me from the inner part of the woods, the top of a thicket, or the surface of a hill. My apparitions were always still, and their words delivered amicably with composure. They always spoke to me like this: "Hey you, you need to be unhappy. Very unhappy, okay? And you need to experience suffering, because unhappiness and suffering are home to the human soul."

But, I had no idea what I should take up to make myself feel suffering. I had little sex drive, so not being with a woman wouldn't cause me to suffer. What part of me, exactly, should do the suffering? So, I tried to imagine what it would be like to be unhappy: Poverty. Illness. A broken heart. Failing in ambition. Old age. Ignorance. Being in a feud. Despair. I was completely satisfied. I groped for unhappiness, and yet I could not even grasp the shadow of it. Even my memory of being a naughty child afraid of reprimand and entirely disconsolate, was something that provided me with more of a nostalgic feeling than any sense of past suffering. What is unhappiness?

Nonetheless, the intermittent appearance of those shadows of myself gradually weighed heavily on me. I considered going to a house of ill-repute, and wondered, "Could it help if I catch the filthiest and the most horrible sexually transmitted disease?"

There was a girl, Suzuki, in my class. It was a well-known fact that her older sister had a husband-and-wife type relationship with her biological father. The darkness of sin at that house fell upon this child's personality and cast a dismal shadow; she rarely talked with friends and never once did she play cheerfully. She always stayed in the corner looking despondent, and when I spoke with her, she'd provide only a weak smile. I sensed no life force to her body.

When I was puzzled by unhappiness, I thought of this twelve-year-old girl's dismal being.

There was also a girl, Ishizu, and another girl, Yamada. I sometimes doubted whether those two were not physically already women. Ishizu, had an alluring quality about her, and when speaking with me, displayed a certain coquettish demeanor, yet, in spite of that quality, compared to other female students, was in possession of the least amount of petty malice; I feel, in the end, all she will be left with is a voluptuous body others will trifle with. This one too had few friends, and by nature seemed without concern for building the clique-like fences a lot of other girls were inclined to construct. Regardless, she was cheerful and always laughing and had the look of someone vacantly staring, mouth-agape.

Yamada was a child from a tofu selling family, but she wasn't the offspring of both parents; she was the child of the wife from a previous marriage. Her younger sister and brother were the family's biological children. The girl was one of those who couldn't write any words but her full name in simple

WIND, LIGHT, AND THE TWENTY-YEAR-OLD ME

Japanese characters and was physically the strongest among the girls. She fought boys with equal verve, and few could beat her. She had a big frame. Her lips were always tightly pursed and her face had a rather intelligent look about it. Gloom wasn't a defining characteristic; she looked like she was brooding over something, with no liveliness in her and no friends at all. Rarely did she speak with others, as if she didn't find joy in speaking, but still, silently participated in playground activities and was very untamed running about. She rarely laughed, or didn't seem to find anything fun, but compared to other children, her jumping around was filled with intensity and a wild animal-like force, and cut a markedly expansive, forceful groove. And yet, allure, she lacked. She appeared to be bold and fearless, but realistically I found the intrinsic fearlessness that resides in all women to be more plentiful in other piddly little girls; she held scant feelings of jealousy or wickedness characteristic of women. And, while she may have appeared to be ripening early, I believed when all these children became adults, she would be the last to reach womanhood, be left behind, and lose out to all other women.

One night, this girl's mother visited me. She explained the particular circumstances of her daughter's situation that her being the sole biologically unrelated child among her few siblings had given her a warped disposition, and asked me to remonstrate her for not opening up more to her adopted father since there was no particular prejudice on her parents' end. This mother had a reputation for being a lascivious woman, and indeed, by the look of her seemed to *be* a lascivious woman, whose age was around thirty-something. "No, she is not warped," I said, "she only appears to be. She possesses an amenable spirit, and an admirable character that allows her to accurately discern and adopt what's right. There is no need for my remonstrance. True love from the both of you is the question that needs to be addressed. What worries me most is that your daughter has so little potential to be loved by others—so little potential to be loved as a woman. It's not that she's warped. It's true, isn't it, that no one has ever really loved your daughter? Foremost, her parents? You and your husband? Asking me to give her a sermon is entirely off the mark. Why don't you yourself ask your own heart?"

The mother, inscrutable, listened to my words, obscure and incoherent in expression. I supposed she too was yet another who couldn't write anything but her name in *kana*. She was, though, entirely amorous and alluring, the complete opposite of her child. Bottom line, she was a woman. The mother and daughter's only shared disposition was the lascivious, animalistic nature of the mother and the daughter's wild nature. The daughter was built large, but the mother, very tiny. Their faces each fell under the category of good looking. For a few minutes, the woman remained quiet, then after engaging in small talk in an overly friendly manner, soon went home.

Along with Suzuki, I was frequently reminded of Ishizu and Yamada. I cannot help but think the future holds only unhappiness for these three. My initial gaze into what unhappiness was came not from my own relation to unhappiness, but from above the students' gloom. This unhappiness means one is not loved; one is not respected. In the case of Ishizu, she would merely be toyed with, and I imagined a worthless lump of flesh soon living as a prostitute lacking various emotions like joy, anger, sadness, or pleasure. I didn't know a real brothel or a prostitute, and I only constructed my reality based on what I gained through novels and other sorts. But I'm still positive my presentiment was correct.

Ishizu was the daughter of a poor family, and lice swarmed about her body. Other kids brought attention to it and teased her. Her face would turn tense in anger but soon again ease up into an innocent smile. Her soul felt foolish rather than virtuous. Nonetheless, she could read and write, and her grades were about average, but in treading the path of life, she lacked the knowledge to navigate the world when compared to women who didn't master hiragana or katakana; in short, this foolish soul of hers, from which one cannot expect true growth, was peeping out and on display. And yet, there was this alarming sexiness about her. Nothing more.

When I left the profession, I thought of inheriting this girl as a maid and taking her with me. If a natural consequence eventually connected two bodies, I wouldn't mind getting married. It was indeed a strange delusion. Still today, I'm oddly attracted to idiotic women, and this was the beginning of that reality; I was not cognizant of matters like love for another or fire in the heart, I was of calm mind, and absorbed in the thought that I could marry this girl in the future.

I've entirely forgotten the face, even its contours, of the noble female teacher and don't have a way to picture it in my mind, but I remember the faces of those three girls as vividly as if they were right here in front of me. I feel like Ishizu would always be vulnerably delicate, and optimistically untroubled even if she was toyed with, stamped upon, and abused mercilessly, but nonetheless that would certainly not be the case in reality because when made fun of and called "lice swarm" she'd turn stern-faced and flash her eyes wide, summoning anger for a second; it leaves me imagining her being trampled upon in the street like horseshit, suffering and gasping for breath. My hunch has proven to be correct; when interacting with prostitutes in brothels later in life, I would often encounter fragile optimists like that.

These days, I have come to think that every man experiences his greatest level of maturity during the period when he changes from young man to adult.

There are two young men who have been coming to visit me lately on occasion. Both are twenty-two, hard-boiled ultranationalists with a history of belonging to right-wing organizations, but now appear to be thinking about a truer way for a man to live his life. Although they can somewhat understand that my "Discourse on Decadence" and "Discourse on Fall" are words of truth, because of the extreme nature of the writing, these discourses remain difficult to follow. These young men revere moderation most of all.

There is another pair of young men, both having just returned from the war: one a poet, and the other an editor who belonged to a suicide squad during the war. They occasionally stay over my house for a few nights and cook me meals making clankety-clank sounds along the way; these two men carry shadows of the battlefield. A rough, untamed, wild nature gained from having been on the front brims from within. However, they possess a surprisingly moderate quality in their souls; that is to say, they too hold dear a trace of their own graceful female teacher. Both are also twenty-two. They have not begun a life of true lust yet. Their minds may not have matured to the age where the physical needs of the body cause suffering. Men of this age, though, are more mature than men of forty or fifty. Their moderate nature comes naturally to them and is not fabricated, forced, or twisted like that of an older man. For a certain period in life, I think, every man is an optimist like Candide. Then they fall and become decadent. But, I assume most lose purity in their souls as their bodies become more decadent.

Later in life, I would read Voltaire's Candide and smile wryly; when I was a teacher, I was chased by my vague inclination toward unhappiness and suffering, but in reality, I could only grasp unhappiness and suffering as fancy ideas. At the time, as a way to grant myself unhappiness, I would think of going to brothels and wonder about falling ill with the filthiest and most horrible disease. Strangely, this idea would entwine itself round my mind in entrenched fashion. Nothing too concerning. It may be because I couldn't imagine what unhappiness was beyond these options.

While a teacher, I did not experience the common pain of navigating life as an employee: no clashing with bosses, being bullied, or subject to the friction of cliques. There were only five of us. And there was no way we could have possibly had a clique even if we wanted to. It was a branch school, and because the head teacher was not the principal, he did not have much sense of responsibility; he was very irresponsible to begin with and had no passion for education whatsoever. Neglecting his class, he busily ran around doing things like playing matchmaker for the influential man, and so he was never able to say anything to anybody about the education profession, not one iota; even though I used a slightly slanted curriculum that lacked music and an abacus-focused math class (because I was horrible in both subjects) he did not complain. Only, once in a blue moon, he'd pull me aside and hint that I must take very good care of the children of influential families. But I didn't get hung up on those things nor did I feel any further need to act on the head teacher's hint since I loved all my students equally.

A landowner's son, Ogiwara, was the child the head teacher told me to give special attention to; this landowner was a school board member. A good kid by nature, though he was sometimes mischievous; I'd sometimes have to scold him for his mischief, but he knew well why he was being reprimanded, and seemed rather secure and calm when I'd forgive him afterward. One day, he started crying. "You only scold me, none of the others!" he said in tears. This wasn't true. In reality, he was just a spoiled boy who wanted to be pampered by me. "Oh, is that so? Do I really single you out for scolding?" I said and started laughing. He stopped crying at once, and started laughing as well. The head teacher failed to recognize this kind of connection between me and my children.

Children are sly creatures just like adults. For example, the milk house boy who flunked and had to repeat the same grade was sly alright, but at the same time, there was right courage residing within him, and he'd acceptingly sacrifice himself for others; it boils down to this worthy distinction in right courage that separates children from adults. It's greater in children than in adults. Children can't help being sly. Being sly is not a vice, and it coexists with right courage; when the proper amount of right courage no longer exists in harmony with slyness, that, I thought, was a problem.

One day after school, the students and teachers had all left, and vacantly absorbed in thought alone in the staff room, I heard someone knocking on the glass window from outside. It was the head teacher.

Earlier, on his way home, he had stopped by the Ogiwaras, and witnessed the Ogiwara boy's tear-filled return from school; the boy told his father and the head teacher he'd been scolded by me. "It's all your fault, father! Because you're throwing your weight around being a school board member. That's why my teacher hates me! Father, it's your fault. You fool!" the boy said, acting so unruly and so out of control. The head teacher asked, "Why on earth did you scold him?"

Little did he know, I didn't…. Children act out because they're sad; invariably, there is meaning behind their actions, therefore, we should never judge a child's actions by what we see on the surface. "I see…," I told the head teacher. "It wasn't extremely bad behavior, but I had to teach him a lesson or two, so I did what I needed to do." "Alright, then," the head teacher smiled obsequiously. "Why don't you take a quick trip to the Ogiwaras now and explain what really happened? As we say: *If you can't beat them, join them.* Conformity brings about a better consequence. We cannot help it, right? Hehe." The head teacher was a man who often ended his words with this chuckling, "hehe."

"I don't need to go. Would you please tell the boy, and only the boy, to come here on your way back home?"

"Alright. But hey, you cannot scold your children too much."

"Yes, I know… but they are my children, so please leave them up to me."

"Alright. But please make sure you adjust your tone of reprimand. Especially with the children of influential families."

The head teacher was probably in good spirits, so he took my words more readily than expected and hopped away. I had forgotten until today that he had this way of walking with his butt sticking out sideways and hopping because he was a bit lame. Those feet, however, were awfully fast.

Soon the boy came into view, smiling in embarrassment; he called my name from outside the window and hid himself. Although I scolded him often, he was my favorite kid, and well understood my deep affection for him.

"Why did you give your father trouble?"

"Because I was very irritated."

"Tell me the truth. You engaged in mischief on the way home from school, didn't you?"

The troubles and agony children lock in their hearts are persistent and serious just as with adults, and perhaps even more so with children. Just because the reasons for their troubles are childish, we cannot conclude the depth of their agony is infantile. The degree of self-reproach and anguish is the same for everyone regardless of age, whether a boy of seven or a man of forty.

The boy started crying. Apparently, from the outside display table of the stationary store next to the school, he had lifted a pencil. The milk house boy, Tanaka, had threatened him and made him do it; perhaps Tanaka had a secret that made Ogiwara vulnerable and he took advantage of it. Nevertheless, I did not need to meddle and ask all the details between the two; in any case, Ogiwara reluctantly stole the pencil. I told him, "Don't worry. I'll pay for the pencil without revealing your name." He went home pleased. A few days later, carefully checking nobody else was around, he slid into the staff room, pulled out twenty or thirty sen, and asked, "Teacher, did you already pay?"

As far as the milk house boy goes, every time he sensed he'd be scolded after his bad conduct came to light, he would start working with extreme diligence. He'd volunteer to be in charge of cleaning duty; busily, he'd even wipe the window glass. Or, he'd say: "Teacher, the toilet seems full now, so, I'll go and draw the waste." "You can do that?" I'd say. "I can do anything that requires manual labor!" "Alright. But where are you going to bring the waste?" "I'll dump it into the river behind the school." "Don't be ridiculous."

Generally, this was how it would go. I found it extremely

comical because once again, he began his routine of diligence just as I would have expected.

I walked toward him. He edged back at once.

"Teacher…! No, please, don't scold me!"

He covered his ears with all his might and closed his eyes.

"No, I won't scold you."

"Will you forgive me?"

"Yes, I'll forgive you. Now, you can't put others up to stealing stuff anymore. If you can't help but do bad things, don't use others. Act on your own. Good or bad, you've got to do things on your own."

Tanaka would always listen, nodding his head.

If one considered what we preached to young children as life's precepts worth following, he would find the occupation of teaching hollow, and the idea of continuing with it, impossible. When young, however, I was confident about myself. I couldn't possibly imagine preaching to children like that now in a million years. In those days, however, I was senselessly absorbed in how it was that nature made me feel, and from within my soul, something like a hymn to the sun forever poured and played. I somehow remained completely and unblushingly void of desire and ignorant to the true emptiness that comes from being in that state. Staying there was entirely possible.

When I quit my teaching job, I was irresolute. Why must I quit? I had decided to study Buddhism and become a monk, longing for enlightenment and a sense of nostalgia for the discipline required to attain enlightenment. Eventually I realized, though, that this same disciplined quality could be pursued and used in life as a teacher. With that realization, I came to understand fame was what I truly desired, not enlightenment, and lamented over this self-seeking lowly desire. I was devoid of hope. The fruition of my aspiration for discipline and enlightenment rested upon a need to renounce the world, and yet, deep down in my heart, I feared this idea; my sense of remorse, despair, and anxiety continued, and came from the knowledge that I was abandoning right hope. "What I was doing must not have been enough. I need to discard anything and everything. And, only after that, might I be able to grasp a way out." I was observant of myself being single-mindedly impatient with discarding. I was like a desperate madman: discard, discard, discard—discard everything no matter what it may be. Just like committing suicide is one means of desire to live, my desperate orientation toward discarding was actually nothing more than the green spring of my youth going pitter-patter behind me. That I knew as well. You see, I had wanted to become a novelist since I was a young boy. But I convinced myself I did not possess the talent. This deeply entrenched belief that had me give up right hope altogether could be what fundamentally drove me to madness and desperation.

Looking back and examining my history during my year as a teacher, strangely and completely satisfied, I feel as though that person was someone else; every time I think about it, it feels like a lie—an inexplicably transparent falsehood.

---

[1] This is our translation for the title, "Jinshin Shūranjutsu" (人心收攬術). Although Ango says he translated this boxing novel, researchers have not uncovered reference to such a title in their review of past *Shinseinen* editions. The translation may have ended up being withheld from publication or published in a different magazine. As noted in the Ango chronology (year, 1922) on the Niigata City Art & Culture Promotion Foundation's Ango Digital Museum website. (https://ango-museum.jp/history/chronology/)

[2] The School of Overseas Colonial Migration (海外植民学校): established in 1916 for the purpose of preparing Japanese students for their eventual migration to South America.

[3] *Neko* (for cat), *jita* (for tongue): describes someone who has trouble eating food served at too hot a temperature, in the same way a cat dislikes food that is too hot.

AFTERTALK

Doc (D) and Reiko (R)

"We were definitely glad to be finished, I think."

D: So do you want to start? You usually have good things to say in the beginning. Did you enjoy this work?

R: Um… it's complicated… I enjoyed it of course, but as time went, it started dragging and dragging, and so towards the end, I just wanted it to end.

D: We were definitely glad to be finished, I think. After a while I was so deep into editing, and thinking about it only as a piece of writing that needed to be edited, that I stopped being familiar with the storyline and began confusing all these different elements… especially with the whole rural school thing. So many damn schools to keep track of… he was in a rural school, then he was in Tokyo, but in a rural area, at a different school… and I remember asking… "like, wait, did he teach at the same school?" [laughter] I think I need to be away from it for a month or so, so I can actually enjoy it as a story.

AFTERTALK

R: It happens a lot for you. Especially this one. It gets confusing even for me too, especially the last paragraph. I remember I had to map out the logic of his thought process, and I had to spend some time with it. In the very beginning I was getting mad at you because you kept forgetting things I thought were essential, and core to his philosophy, like in that section where you were asking me if he'd ever referred to this idea of "right hope," when we had talked about it so many times.

D: Ah, yeah… that's me with my editor hat on completely forgetting about what came before the last sentence. There, I'm just focusing on the words and the rhythm for the most part. It's easy for me to forget, though, and especially when Ango is jumping back and forth with people he's *just* introduced me to like Yamada and Ishizu… I'll ask you, "Is this the fat girl?" Then on top of that, he also uses the same damn word to describe different people… oh my God.

R: Yeah in those parts, you seemed confused. But, yeah, this story is different in a way from other stories we've translated. We published the abridged version first, then decided to complete the whole story a year later. What you were saying the other day, which was an interesting point, was that the story made sense in the abridged version but in the unabridged version things were made even more clear after we added what we'd previously taken out.

D: Right. So I like this story even in its abridged form because I like that it's philosophical. And once we completed the unabridged version, that aspect of the story made even more sense. It was nice to see how Ango thought about things and how he articulated those ideas, especially in those last two pages. Still, even though you had cut things out in the abridged version, I got a lot out of it, and it has remained my favorite story. It made sense. You were able to walk away from that version with the meaning intact. It was such a good job, I think, of selectively cutting things.

R: Thank you.

D: It's amazing actually how well you're able to do that. I'm guessing you never did that before, so that was pretty darn cool. But then this time, because we can see the entire story, we gain insight into *why* it was that he was able to be so philosophical, or rather, how he got away from being *just* philosophical.

R: What do you mean?

D: In the unabridged version we see now that he actually does come up with an answer to what unhappiness is, right? He's so comfortable in life in most of the early part of the story and then he meets these girls and he realizes, "Oh, this is what unhappiness is." I don't know… it's still… even just talking about it now… it's still a complicated idea. I've also been thinking lately that it's not actually a *story*. I mean, it's just like he's telling…

R: Yeah, but this is his style of telling a story. He uses his experience to create a story that helps the reader benefit. I have a collection of similar types of stories—biographical-type novels.

D: Autobiographical, you mean?

R: Yes, autobiographical, although they're not completely autobiographical. He uses his experience, but still, it's modified as if it were a novel… I guess as an artist he takes poetic license with things, so the story acts as a piece of literature, highlighting what he sees as important to make the scene more meaningful… just like Dazai (in *Wish Fulfilled*). It's just a woman skipping, but he paints it as this beautiful moment that goes beyond that and leaves an impression in the reader's mind. In the research I did, I found out he mostly used real people in this story... there was that website I was showing you... remember? With the names of his colleagues? And you could see that he had used the real names of those people in the story. You could also see he registered with the school as a teacher using his pen name, Ango; when his real name was Heigo.

D: Really?

R: Yes. He registered his name as Sakaguchi Ango. But the person who was sharing this website couldn't identify who the beautiful female teacher might have been. I don't know... Ango might have created that character for the purpose of this story. We also don't know about those three girls; it's very likely that he had these three girls as students, but again we don't know if he created them, or...

D: It could be like a composite of people too; so basically you take characteristics of many people and wrap those traits into one person. So we don't know who the noble teacher was, or whether she was a real person, but didn't the people who created this website read interviews with him and stuff so that might have been discovered somehow? Didn't he ever talk about any of these things, or wasn't he ever interviewed about these stories?

R: It seems like he did some interviews but not about this story in particular. Probably writers don't want to talk about their work once it's done. They want to move on.

"Do you remember that horseshit part?"

D: Yeah, that's often true. Is there a certain part of this story that you really enjoyed?

R: For the unabridged version, I especially like the addition of those sections with the female students. We worked very hard, and spent a lot of time on those parts—on those three girls. I'm quite proud of those sections. Like Yamada's part... my initial translation of one of the words he uses to describe Yamada's force was "beast-like." And you convinced me it might not be the best choice, especially because later on we had to draw a comparison between her and the sexy mother. And then with Yamada's mother, there's this descriptive adjective that Ango used to describe the mother's face; that word in Japanese wouldn't typically be used to describe a face. It would be used to describe a piece of writing... or, a talk, or an idea. But because he used it to describe a person's face, we had to spend time figuring out how to deliver it in the right way using English.

D: Yeah, there were certainly a number of words and sentences that we really had to wrestle with in this story... more than Nakjima and Dazai for sure.

R: Do you remember that horseshit part? You were so certain the word order of that sentence was off, because you said, "Horsehit don't gasp for breath." [laughter]

D: Ah, yes... the original translation we had was something like, "she'd be stepped on in the street and gasping for breath like horseshit." As if horseshit had the ability to breathe. Which ain't possible. But, that's the order of it in the original, right?

R: Yes. No matter how flexible I allow myself to be, that's almost the only way it can be read.

D: Nuts. So, aside from all this word wackiness, what was the trickiest part overall would you say?

R: Uh, maybe the beginning part...

D: Yeah, that sucked.

R: [laughter] It was interesting how you were struggling with the editing because, looking back, the sentences are very simple, or at least in Japanese are quite straightforward. But you wanted the parts to flow nicely, so we had to break things down, and go back and forth, and play with the sentences in so many different ways. And while the sentences we came up with aren't so complex, if you look at the history of our revisions you can see how much of a struggle that was.

D: There must be so many versions. Listening to you talk about this just now, I'm reminded that yes; that's part of the problem with a lot of Japanese, to me at least, and to my ear... and especially him, the way he writes in this kind of staccato style. It's kind of like the difference between *sobameshi* and *soba*. You know sobameshi, right?

R: Sobameshi is... uh, food. [laughter]

D: [laughter] Sobameshi is food, yeah. It's Kansai creation, or maybe it's a Shinnagata area kind of a dish? It's basically soba that's tossed on a grill, almost like *yakisoba*, but a little bit different. It's soba... cooked on a grill... and then chopped up (!) with meat and stuff like that.

R: Ah... ah...

D: So, it's like chopped spaghetti. It's *chopped* soba instead of long *flowy* soba, right? It's just like: *chak, chak, chak, chak...* that's what these sentences were in the beginning.

R: Ah! So, soba acting as rice; *meshi* is rice in Japanese.

D: Yeah, so it's all chopped up. That's the way it felt. And I remember thinking this has to be better because we can't lead with these disgusting sentences; then people will never get past page two.

R: Yeah, that was me wanting to create a framework as a vomit draft; I knew those parts weren't finished and they felt difficult to do on my own... I had many word choices, remember? And I wanted to ask you which words would be best suited for the nuance I felt in Japanese. And, because this time—usually, I translate a handful of sentences, and show you—but this time, I did all the translation on my own at first... writing in a notebook... and then when everything was finished, I showed you.

D: Right, we did do that with the new parts.

R: I thought maybe we could edit together, so I wasn't particularly paying attention to the sentences; I was going through it quickly. Oh! And I want to talk about the finding of semicolons. They were a savior for us.

D: Yeah, we owe Kafka a royalty check.

R: One thing that was difficult about Ango was that his sentences just go on and on; it connects and connects and connects without any periods. So we didn't know how to connect those different ideas into a single long sentence and I remember having difficulty with it. I wanted to use "and," but you didn't like using it so many times, so we had to switch the order of things and use our heads, so everything would fall together nicely. But after finding the semicolon, I was very, very happy.

D: Yeah... yeah, because that opened up everything so we could honor the longer sentences... are they sentences? ...that longer method that he uses. We were able to do that because of the power the semicolon gave us, without having to flip things around and deal with "ANDs" and "ORs." Remember, there were lots of "SOs" in there as well, and I was like, "there are so many friggin SOs." The ways we were trying to get these sentences to make sense in English weren't working. And it all came from Kafka. We were reading and I was like, "Do you notice all the semicolons? This might come in handy." And I wrote about it on Linkedin, or whatever. You were like, "I already got that."

R: It was very good timing to be reading Kafka at this point. Kafka was Czech?

D: He was, yeah. It was also great because he has these sentences that go on and on without a single paragraph break for pages, that really made the semicolon stand out.

R: It was good that we happened to be reading a translated book because we could see the translator's technique in bringing Kafka into English. It's interesting; we found many similarities in these two people we happened to be reading.

"But candor is his strength. He doesn't shy away from things. And, I wonder if this is… I don't know; is this common for men to think about fifth grade girls as women?"

D: For sure—definitely a good find. This story was also interesting because of the way Ango is talking about these young girls; remember, I was having trouble with that. It felt really odd and uncomfortable describing twelve-year-old girls as "alluring" and "alarmingly sexy." Very strange.

R: I thought so too.

D: That's why nobody interviewed him about this. [laughter]

R: [laughter] But candor is his strength. He doesn't shy away from things. And, I wonder if this is… I don't know; is this common for men to think about fifth grade girls as women? Do men think of young girls as women already at that age?

AFTERTALK

When do you start that idea?

D: Oh, no no… not unless you want to end up in prison for the rest of your life. What I think he's getting at, is that maybe they possess certain adult characteristics—this is why we settled on "coquettish"—and why I was spending so much time looking at the definition of that word and how it's applied. I wanted to get a really good feeling for whether I could use that word and not feel embarrassed, or bad, or put him in a bad light if he wasn't trying to say a certain thing.

R: It was a good move because he's not by any stretch of the imagination trying to be overly friendly with them. He's being scientific, in a sense… analyzing them in a scientific way.

D: Right. He's noticing their behavior. That's why "coquettish" works as a word because he's not saying they are women, but he's saying they exhibit certain characteristics that are the kinds of characteristics mature women possess. Sometimes there are younger girls who are a bit ahead of the curve on that sort of thing and that's why that word exists. But, to answer your question, men don't think of young girls as women at that age at all, I think. There are some girls at that age that act like an older woman might, or, as a teenager might, I think. Maybe they have older sisters, or maybe their mother, like in the story—this one girl's mother is described as being lascivious, and kind of sexy—and Ango is picking up on them mimicking that behavior.

R: Wait, are you talking about the mother of Yamada? Yamada isn't the girl who's sexy. Ishizu is. [laughter]

D: Oh that's right. See, that's what I'm talking about, I can't place any of these names and situations. But, um, I think the basic idea holds true, right? Still it was weird to use those words especially when I don't know the whole context of the sentence yet; all I'm getting is "twelve-year-old, sexy, alarming…" and I'm like, "What? This is so weird." But, we figured it out. He's definitely not mincing words. He's talking about… she's going to be stepped on…

R: Yeah, that part is strong. But, um, he's interestingly fascinated by this type of girl, right? Not these exact girls, but this type of women who possess this shadow of sadness but who are idiotic as well. Do you remember when we were translating the conversation with Dazai, Sakaguchi and Oda? And Dazai says, "I want to be in love with a beggar woman." So, Dazai and Sakaguchi probably share the belief that a beggar woman and a prostitute both possess a certain innocence. They have a tough life, and because of that tough life, they maybe have less demands on life. So, in a certain way, that's an attractive quality?

D: You mean they have less desire to be alive or an appreciation of life? What do you mean?

R: Less demanding of a man; more carefree, perhaps. Ango was saying this girl has an almost… about Ishizu…

D: Amenable spirit?

R: Uh, that's Yamada…. [laughter] An optimistic and untroubled soul. He has a certain idea about these—what he calls—idiotic women who have a kind of purity about them.

D: Do you know why? Does he have like a… is there something in his history that suggests he would be attracted to that sort of person other than what we just read? I think maybe that's the answer…

R: Um, I don't know, probably he was disappointed by calculative women in life, so he feels much safer around these less calculative women.

AFTERTALK

D: Yeah, he definitely seems to appreciate the lack of that characteristic in some of these girls. Every man, I would hope, would appreciate that. In the talk with Oda and those guys, what does Sakaguchi say about women?

R: He said… oh, he actually said, "There's nothing intrinsic about them." So, as far as I know, he had this relationship with the writer, Yada Tsuseko—she was kinda popular back then, and he wrote about her in at least three different stories—she may have been the first person who broke his heart. And he was haunted by the memory of her for a long time. When they met, he fell in love with her instantly, and they got along well. They were both this kind of rising-star-type writer and she was beautiful, and he thought maybe they would get married, but it turned out she was having a love affair with an executive staff member of a famous newspaper company. So she was not entirely honest with Ango, and Ango later found out. So, probably, that soured his view on women.

D: Sounds like it for sure. He was writing about her, you said? Where?

R: In different stories: "Nijūnanasai" (Twenty-seven years old), "Sanjussai" (Thirty years old), and "Izuko e" (To where).

D: Really? That's cool. Hmmm. Okay, … uh, what else?

"His writing is very unique, and he doesn't seem to like using periods so he keeps going on and on with his commas."

R: I was glad we went over the original, abridged version again because we changed quite a lot and it got a lot better; I was surprised to find it had room for improvement. It's funny what Kafka's translator (Breon Mitchell) says in his preface… what does he say? It was his dream to translate Kafka and he now dreams of how he could have done it better… or, something like that. It's always true that we can find something worth improving when it comes to our own work.

D: Yeah that's true. I mean, that's the thing, I think we were just making it flow better, or massaging it, and not that things were wrong with the translation—and that was the problem with the boxer page. The boxer page was all like that. We didn't run into that issue with Nakajima and we didn't run into that issue with Dazai. It's just Sakaguchi's style.

R: His writing is very unique, and he doesn't seem to like using periods so he keeps going on and on with his commas.

D: You often like to say he might have been under the influence when he wrote this… [laughter]

R: Yes, I think so. [laughter] When we went over his timeline, we saw that around the time he wrote this piece, he was suffering from an addiction to stimulants and regularly drinking in excess.

D: Mmmm… he likes to repeat words as well…

R: Yeah, so there are four or five appearances of the same word close together.

D: Right. There was that one word that you just kept in there in Japanese, and we came back later to figure it out. Your notes from that part are really cool because you had all the different possibilities we could choose from. I think just that bit of editing probably took two hours or so to figure out which word to put where. I remember that pretty clearly. Yeah, he doesn't like periods for sure, and he likes to repeat things. There are two paragraphs where he was quite literally repeating himself about the, uh… what does he say? Going to the brothel. Yeah, it's almost like word for word, the same sentence.

AFTERTALK

R: That seems to be his crutch word... I don't know if it's intentional or not. He repeats specific situations in different stories as well, but tells them in a slightly different way. I was sharing this, right?

D: Right... Maybe there's another guy who collects snakes, [laughter] but the boxer's name is R instead of S... [laughter] Why does he just get a letter? Everybody else gets a name. They're outed. He just calls this guy "S." [laughter]

R: He might have just forgotten the boxer's name.

"I groped for unhappiness, and yet I could not even grasp the shadow of it." I love that sentence of yours."

D: Why didn't give him a fake name? So funny.... It was pretty cool going to the library to get a feel for what that area might have looked like, no? We were trying to understand the landscape and how he described the trees, and the wheat fields and all that. We were trying to figure out what the hell a copse was, and then I started seeing them everywhere...

R: Yes, we went to the library and we asked the lady at the front desk for books that could show us what Tokyo looked like in the 20's and she came back with these.... these gigantic books from the reserved area.

D: Yeah, they were all super-old and all in black and white with these cool covers on them... and remember they had advertisements in the front and the back? Underwriters, I suppose, of the book. That was pretty cool.

R: It's amazing how different Tokyo looks now... I couldn't possibly imagine pit vipers slithering around in a swamp in Tokyo.

D: Yeah, everything was just so wide open... even the

AFTERTALK

Nihonbashi area was super rural looking. Amazing. Okay. So, no more Ango for a while?

R: Not for a while. Do you have a favorite sentence?

D: I think my favorite sentences are still from the abridged version, uh… "I groped for unhappiness, and yet I could not even grasp the shadow of it." I love that sentence of yours. But then there's that idea he's sharing—where he's talking about how the pain that kids suffer is similar to the pain suffered by a man of forty—and he uses this word, or, we chose to use this word: "infantile." There's so much poetry in that sentence. Those two sentences are lovely. I also love the way he's describing one of the girls—I think you like this part too—where he says his fear for the girl is whether she's ever really going to be loved, whether she's ever going to be loved as a woman. I really like the rhythm of that. You can tell he really cares about the kid, and he's just a kid himself, really, and he's putting himself up against this parent who seems like she has a pretty complicated life. I like that chutzpah.

"Ango, to me, is multi-dimensional and complex. He seems to be all over the place, doing wild stuff, and his lifestyle represents a sort of decadence… but at the same time, he seems to have a warm heart, and be a very humane person, and knows the true value of life."

R: That part shows how thoughtful and humanistic he is.

D: I also like when he makes a joke, almost, out of the idea of being able to give advice to kids. As if, who are we to give advice to kids and, how silly is that? But I don't really find it so silly, honestly, and I feel that he's dispensing good advice. I love when he talks to the milk house boy and he's telling him, "If you're gonna do bad stuff do it on your own," kinda telling him: "You gotta be a man."

R: His point in the end where he says he can't give young

children that kind of advice anymore is that, when he was young, he was confident and didn't doubt himself. He repeats the concept of moderation and maturity in young men; when you are young, you are more confident and filled with hope— you think you know everything, but you don't, because you haven't experienced true desperation or a feeling of failure. But once you do start experiencing the ugliness of life, you lose confidence in your understanding of it, are stripped of hope and start falling into decadence. Then, when you sense your soul has become decadent, you notice emptiness in it. So that's why he's saying, now around the age forty, giving kids that kind of advice would sound, and feel, fake to him.

D: He's saying it would be hypocritical. And he wouldn't be able to back it up with the sort of belief and passion that he had as a youngster. He would know he's, as we would say, "talking through his teeth." You picked this particular story... why?

R: This story grabbed me and caught my attention.

D: Because of the theme?

R: I don't know... I was interested in Ango himself first; he seems very true to himself and I like how different he is from other typical author-type people. Ango, to me, is multi-dimensional and complex. He seems to be all over the place, doing wild stuff, and his lifestyle represents a sort of decadence... but at the same time, he seems to have a warm heart, and be a very humane person, and knows the true value of life. This "fire" part within him is contrasted by this cool, "cold water" characteristic. And, I can sense there is this kind of cool-headed, tranquil, calm, nature about him. I think that part of him is represented well in this story. In that last paragraph, he's self-critical. He could have ended the story about how passionate he was, or wrap things up with him teaching a life-lesson to the milk house boy, but he comes back to himself as a forty years old, reflective and self-critical. That part is cool. This fire and water within him is intriguing.

D: Indeed. It seems as though his wife was able to see through this fire side of him as well. That passage you shared with me from James Dorsey's book—where he pulled out that section from her diary—referencing her first visit to his house, and it was filled with all that crap all over the floor, papers, and checks, and DDT powder everywhere… and yet, not a spec of food in all that clutter. He seemed to be quite an enigma. Caring so much, but not caring at all. You can see this care he has for others close to him when she's in the hospital as well. He never leaves her side, right? Or even that little bit about him and his brother moving around in Tokyo with their old wet nurse that you drew up for the timeline on the website. There's something to that story too. Who's still living with their wet nurse as an adult? [laughter] I really liked learning about Ango, and working on this story with you. As I keep saying, it remains my favorite. So, thank you for introducing him to my life. And, thank you for your patience in dealing with my forgetfulness as we worked through the whole thing. Thankfully, you're not fiery like Ango. [laughter]

R: [laughter] Well, thank you too for being patient; it took a lot of time even on the final edits. A lot of editing, and recording. We wanted to record your reading so we could listen to the whole thing, and you read the whole story many, many times. Thank you for doing that. As a result, we're able to come up with the one we're proud of.

D: I think so too. Nice work. All right. So that's it until next time…

AFTERTALK

For more English translations of Japanese literary classics, and new releases from Japan's modern storytellers, visit Maplopo.com. You may also wish to consider joining the free Maplopo Reading Circle. We'll send you short stories free, as well as audiobook goodies and other treats from the Maplopo family. Thanks again for reading!

Maplopo

THE LIFE OF SAKAGUCHI ANGO

1906   October 20: Sakaguchi Ango is born in Nishi-Ōhatachō, Niigata as the fifth son of Niichirō and Asa Sakaguchi's nine children—the twelfth overall out of thirteen. Ango's birth name is Heigo. His mother's family, Yoshida, is a powerful landowner. His father, a member of the Diet in the Lower House of Representatives, is president of Niigata Shinbun-sha, and board chairman of Niigata Rice and Grains Stock Exchange Company; he is also a poet of classical Chinese poetry in the Mori Shuntō style.

1913   Enters elementary school. Righteous minded, Ango is a ringleader of kids with an abundant sense of justice. Throughout his six years of elementary school, his grades have always been high, placing him second or third to the top of class. He is appointed to the equivalent of the dean's list each year. He is good at sports as well, and performs honorably at the city's *sumō* wrestling and sports festivals.

1919   Enters Niigata Junior High School. Begins reading novels written by Akutagawa Ryūnosuke and Tanizaki Junichirō, but at the time is more fond of reading sports magazines.

1922   Expelled from junior high school in the summer of his third year on account of punching a teacher.

Transferred to Busan Secondary School in Tokyo. Becomes close friends with Yamaguchi Shūzō and Sawabe Tatsuo. Often sits in Zen meditation with the philosophy-minded Sawabe.

1923   His passion for creative writing deepens with increasing amounts of reading. Reads the works of Anton Chekhov, Masamune Hakucyō, and Satō Haruo often. Among his favorites are Edgar Allan Poe, Charles Baudelaire, and Ishikawa Takuboku. Interested in books on religion and natural philosophy as well. On November 2nd, his father dies of retroperitoneal tumor.

1925   Graduates from Busan Secondary School and becomes a substitute teacher at the Shimokitazawa branch of Ebara Jinjyō Elementary School.

1926   Resigns his position as substitute teacher. Enters Tōyō University as a student in the philosophy and ethics department. Lives around the Ikebukuro area moving from one place to another with his older brother, Hozue, and his aged wet nurse. Immerses himself in the reading of books about Buddhism and philosophy in an attempt to achieve a state of enlightenment. Makes it a rule to wake up at two in the morning each day as part of ascetic training.

1927   Hit by a car, and suffers a skull fracture. Symptoms of depression gradually start to show. Constantly suffers from auditory hallucination and tinnitus, and has difficulty walking. Throughout the fall and winter, pays a daily visit to his friend, Sawabe Tatsuo, who is hospitalized for mental illness at Sugamo Sanatorium.

1928   Becomes an enthusiastic language learner. Learns

Sanskrit, Pali, and Tibetan all at once. In April, enters a language school, Athénée Français, and learns French and Latin too. Is fond of novels by Poe, Baudelaire and Beaumarchais and focuses on reading French literature. Among Japanese writers, Kasai Zenzō, Uno Kōji, Arishima Takerō are his favorites. Reading Chekhov's "A Dreary Story" inspires him, and he writes a novel for the first time at the age of twenty two. Submits the work to *Kaizō*'s prize competition but loses.

1930   Graduates from Tōyō University. That summer, begins planning for the publication of a self-published magazine with friends from Athénée Français, as a way to share their own works with people of similar beliefs and ideas. Among those friends are Kuzumaki Yoshitoshi, Eguchi Kiyoshi, Nagashima Atsumu, Wakazono Seitarō. They work together doing translations at Kuzumaki's every day of the week, all night long. In November, their magazine, *Kotoba*, is launched. Ango serves as co-editor and co-publisher with Kuzumaki.

1931   Publishes his first ever novel, "Kogarashi no sakaba kara" (From a sake warehouse in the winter's wind) in the second issue of *Kotoba*. In May, changes the name of the magazine to *Aoi uma* and publishes its first issue under Iwanami Shoten. Hishiyama Shūzō joins as a new member. In June and July, Ango's "Kaze hakase" (Professor Blowhard) and "Kurotani mura" receive rave reviews from Makino Shinichi, making Ango's name instantly familiar to those in literary circles. In October, his serialized novel "Takeyabu no ie," begins its run in *Bunka* for which Makino is an editor. From that point forward, he gets better acquainted with *Bunka* members such as Kawakami Tetsutarō, Nakajima Kenzō, Kobayashi

Hideo, and Miyoshi Tatsuji.

1932 With an introduction from Kawakami Tetsutarō, Ango visits Ōoka Shōhei in Kyōto. Rents a room in an apartment from Ōoka's friend, Katō Hidemichi, for a month. In the fall, makes Nakahara Chūya's acquaintance in a bar, Windsor, located around the Kyōbashi station in Tokyo as well as, waitress, Sakamoto Mutsuko, and comes to know her quite well.

1933 Meets rising novelist, Yada Tsuseko, falls in love, and enters into a relationship with her. In March, Yada invites Ango to join the self-published magazine, *Sakura*, where he helps with its launch. Among its members are: Tamura Taijirō, Inoue Tomoichirō, Masugi Shizue, and Kawata Seiichi. Around this time, Ango lends a hand organizing the plans for *Kigen*, another self-published magazine, incubated by Oki Kazuichi and Wakazono Seitarō; he then gets Nakahara Chūya to join in. In April, crushed once he discovers Yada Tsuseko is having a love affair with Wada Hidekichi, an executive staff member of Jijishinpō (a newspaper company). In July, Yada is taken into custody by the Special Higher Police for ten days (on suspicion of providing the Japanese Communist Party with monetary support).

1936 Receives a letter from Yada Tsuseko in March; the letter proposes she and Ango break off their relationship completely. That same month, Makino Shinichi (who played a part in Ango being recognized, *see 1931*) commits suicide; Ango later attends Makino's funeral. In June, sends his last letter to Yada Tsuseko.

1940   Meets Ōi Hirosuke on New Year's Eve, and agrees to join Ōi's self-published magazine, *Gendai bungaku*.

1941   Spends days and days at Ōi Hirosuke's having fun playing guessing games where the criminals of detective novels need to be correctly guessed by the members of *Gendai bungaku*, including: Hirano Ken, Sasaki Kiichi, Ara Masahito, Minamikawa Jun, and Inoue Tomoichirō.

1942   In February, Ango's mother, Asa, passes away. In March, he publishes "Nihon bunka shikan" (A personal view of Japanese culture) in *Gendai bungaku*. In June, publishes "Shinju" (Pearls) in *Bungei*.

1944   Becomes a temporary employee at Nippon Eiga Sha (a movie company) to avoid being drafted. In March, Yada Tsuseko passes away.

1946   In April, publishes "Darakuron" (Discourse on decadence), and in June, "Hakuchi" (The idiot), both in *Shinchō*. They attract major attention, instantly making him a popular writer. To deal with a flood of requests for writing, Ango regularly uses methamphetamine and drinks alcohol in excess. On November 22, he attends a meeting along with Dazai Osamu, Oda Sakunosuke, and Hirano Ken, designed to facilitate a discussion about contemporary novels, and three days later on November 25, does another round-table discussion with Dazai and Oda. In December, attends Doyōkai (Saturday meeting) hosted by Edogawa Ranpo.

1947   Publishes "Kaze to hikari to hatachi no watashi to" (Wind, light, and the twenty-year-old me) in *Bungei*, and "Watashi wa umi o dakishimeteitai" (I want to be holding the sea) in *Fujin gahō*. On January 10, Oda Sakunosuke dies of tuberculosis. In March, meets his future wife, Michiyo. In April, publishes "Ren'airon" (Discourse on love) in *Fujin kōron*. Around this time, Michiyo suffers from peritonitis and an emergency operation is performed; Ango attends to Michiyo for one month in the hospital, never leaving her side. After being discharged from the hospital, Michiyo begins to live at Sakaguchi's, gradually recuperating. Publishes "Sakura no mori no mankai no shita" (In the forest, under cherries in full bloom) in *Nikutai*. Ango's first detective novel, which is serialized, "Furenzoku satsujin jiken," begins its run in *Nippon shōsetsu*. Continues to take stimulants, including the usage of amphetamine in addition to methamphetamine.

1948   Dazai Osamu and Yamazaki Tomie, having entered into a lovers' suicide pact, throw themselves into the Tamagawa Aqueduct on June 13. Two days later, on June 15, Ango receives the news of their deaths. In July, publishes "Furyō shōnen to kirisuto" (The delinquent boy and Christ) presenting his original theory about Dazai and civilization. Continues to suffer daily from insomnia and takes sleeping pills in excess while carrying on his regular stimulant usage. Both visual and auditory hallucinations appear.

1949   Undergoes a number of crazed fits from an excessive intake of sleeping pills, resulting in such disturbances as Ango jumping from a second floor window and exerting violence on people in his home. In February, hospitalized in the University of Tokyo Hospital neurology ward. In April, receives a notice of property seizure from the tax office due to his tax arrears, and in protest, submits a letter of objection. In August, experiences a recurrence of fits from sleeping pill addiction; held in custody at the police station. In the winter, gets a dog, allowing him to gradually return to a healthy lifestyle through the habit of walking a dog.

1951　In May, sits in on a public hearing of the first trial of the Chatterley case. (The Chatterley case refers to a legal case where the translator, Itō Sei, and the publisher of D. H. Lawrence's novel, *Lady Chatterley's Lover*, are prosecuted under Article 175 of the penal code for distributing obscene documents.) In November, falls into near insanity from taking an excess amount of sleeping pills in one go and orders one hundred bowls of curry rice from a nearby restaurant, and has them delivered to Dan Kazuo's where Ango is currently staying.

1953　In June, travels with Dan Kazuo from Niigata to Matsumoto, Nagano to obtain research material for a magazine project. During the trip, Ango makes a commotion and acts out violently, which results in him being detained in police custody. As soon as he is released, hears news about the birth of his son, Tsunao. Returning from the trip, Ango makes another wild commotion and finds himself back in custody. Later, he submits to city hall a letter of apology to the mayor, and registers his marriage and the birth of his newborn son.

1954　In August, resigns his post as Akutagawa award selection committee member for which he has been a part of for five and a half years, having shown doubt regarding its selection process. In October, goes home to Niigata with his wife and son for a customary memorial service for his parents.

1955　In February, his serialized travelogs, "Ango

shin'nihonfudoki," begins its run in *Chūō kōron*. On February 17, dies of cerebral hemorrhage at home at the age of forty-eight. After Ango's death, "Aoi jūtan" (The blue carpet) is published in *Chūō kōron*.

BIBLIOGRAPHY

Sakaguchi, Ango. Afterword and timeline. *Kaze to hikari to hatachi no watashi to, Izuko e*. Afterword and timeline by Nanakita Kazuto. Tokyo: Iwanami bunko, 2015.

Sakaguchi, Ango. *Furyō shōnen to kirisuto*. Tokyo: Shinchō bunko, 2019.

————. *Literary Mischief: Sakaguchi Ango, Culture, and the War*. Ed. James Dorsey and Doug Slaymaker, trans. James Dorsey. Lanham, Maryland: Lexington Books, 2010.

Printed in Great Britain
by Amazon